HAZMAT POPCORN TEAM

MISSION 1: HOW YELLING AT FRIENDS WON'T GET THE JOB DONE

WRITTEN AND ILLUSTRATED BY
RYAN BURKE

EDITED BY SARAH PATTISON
LAYOUT & DESIGN BY LISA BURKE

Keep Reading Jeremy.
Love you,   Mrs. Apodaca
2020

for Stella, Jack, Takota & Zach(ary)

& Jeremy!

I hope you enjoy this book as much as
I enjoyed making it for you :)
   Stay tuned for MISSION #2!

          XXB

Have you ever wondered where
it goes...

...the popcorn down
around your toes?

It was there before the show,
but where it's gone nobody knows...

Or do they?

What if I told you there was a team
the theater had hired to quarantine...

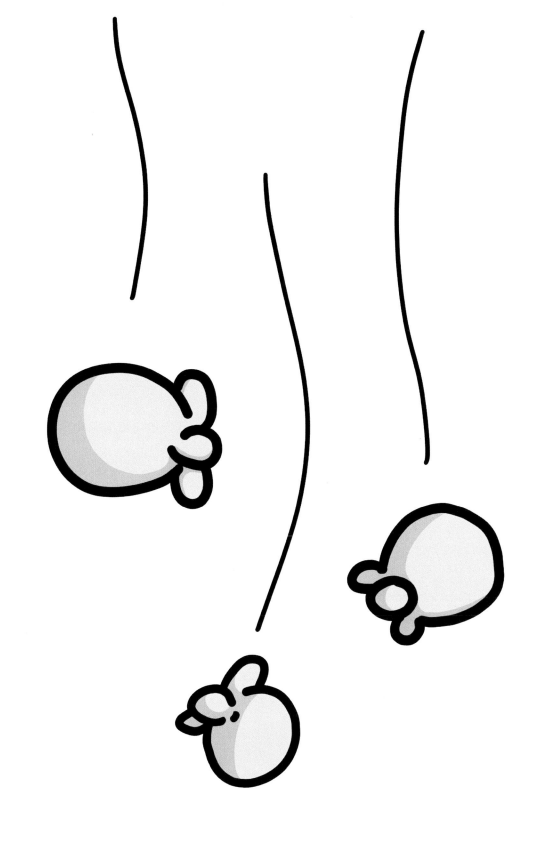

...your very favorite, fluffy treat
the moment it fell down at your feet?

The theater crew has too much to do,
like sell tickets, show movies, and more.

So they trust in these four
to handle one chore,
and get all the popcorn
off of the floor.

Trooper's job is to locate the kernels and pick up along the way.

Though often times his creative mind will lead his attention astray.

Jack has a gift for gathering popcorn and it's really rather neat.

He sets up his bag and shows off his swag by kicking it in with his feet.

Zapp is an ace with his popcorn blaster
and he loves to do one thing.

When there's too much popcorn
for their bags to handle
he blasts it to smithereens.

With one eye on the time
and her duty in mind,
Sarge knows just what to do.

She's in charge of the team,
can get the floors clean,
and won't stop 'til the mission is through.

Every night is a different mission...

...I'll tell you one,
If you care to listen.

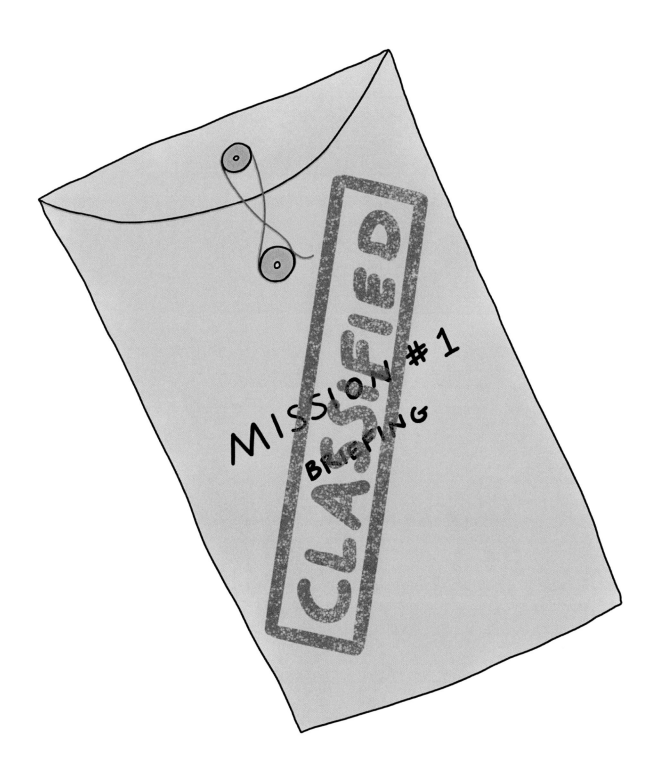

One time Trooper and Jack got distracted.

Sarge, in turn, may have overreacted.

Shhh. Thank you.

"QUIT THAT NONSENSE!"

"PUT THAT DOWN!"

"WE'VE GOT TO GET THIS STUFF OFF THE GROUND!"

"WHAT ARE YOU DOING?

WHY WON'T YOU CLEAN?!"

"We're not helping."

"You're too mean."

"BE THAT WAY,
WE DON'T NEED YOU TWO!

Zapp and I will have to do."

It wasn't so bad, at first,
without help from Trooper and Jack.

Sarge was just as good at finding popcorn
and getting it into her pack.

"With Zapp on his blaster
and me moving faster
we can easily get the job done.

And whatever we do
when the mission is through,
the others can't join in our fun!"

But even with a popcorn blaster,
the job wasn't going any faster.

The show was ending and there was still a mess...

they'd need the whole team to finish the rest.

"Where in the world are Trooper and Jack? I haven't seen them all night."

"That may be because, when I asked them for help, I wasn't very polite."

"I thought that we could do it all,
without the other two...

But now I see it's too much for me,
and probably too much for you."

"How can I get them to help us finish,
before the show lets out?

They were really upset when I lost my temper
and began to stomp and shout."

"Whatever you do, do it quick
and try to make things right.

If you don't, and it's just us two,
we're not going to finish tonight."

So off she went to make amends,
knowing now that she needed her friends.

She couldn't think of what to say...
she thought and thought the entire way.

"Yelling will not help me lead, the others
will not want to listen.

I'll need to try another approach
to see if they'll continue the mission."

"HEY!!

I mean--Hi.
I yelled at you and don't know why."

"I'm sorry for the way I acted
when you two became distracted.

This mission's important, but so are you…
and we'll need your help to see it through."

"From here on out I promise you both
to keep my temper at rest,
and use my energy positively
to encourage you to do your best."

This sounded like a better plan
compared to what happened before.

So Trooper and Jack decided together
that they were not mad anymore.

They saw that their friend was full of regret,
and knew it was time to forgive and forget.

So with that the team was whole once more...

But there was still so much popcorn on the floor!

"We'll work together to get this done,
and then we'll go and have some fun!"

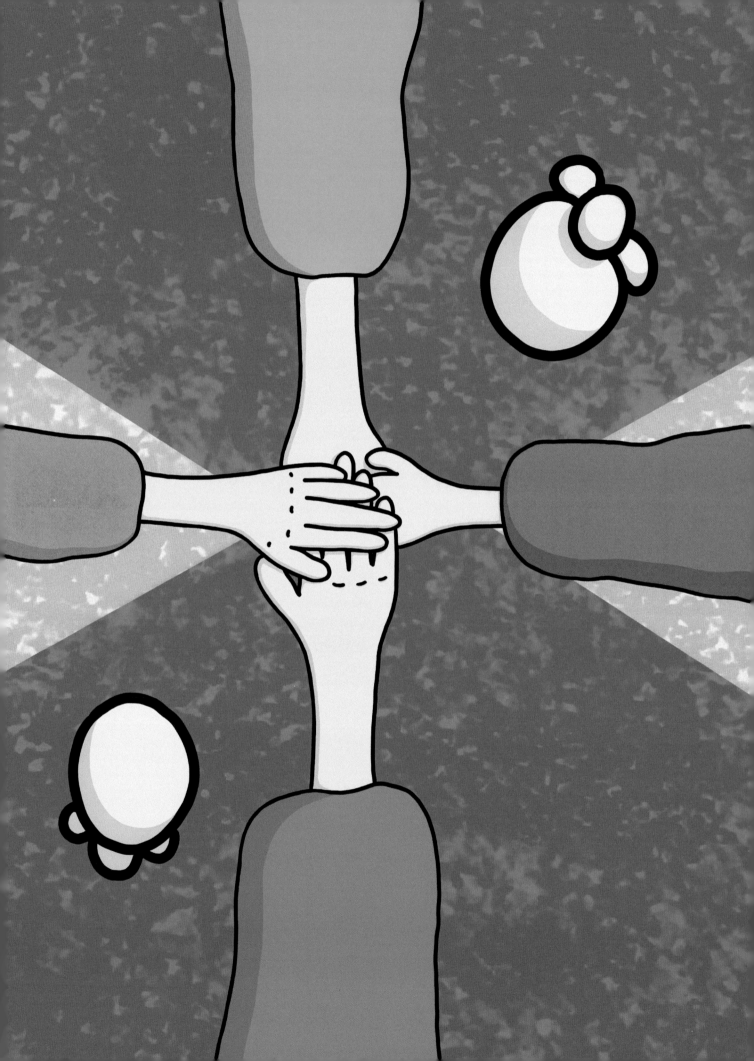

Search, gather, bag and BLAST!
The mission was over in a flash!

The show had ended,
the floors were clean...

...Thanks to Hazmat Popcorn Team!

The end.

Or is it?

Made in the USA
San Bernardino, CA
23 February 2020